The Adventures of
MARY-KATE & ASHLEY™

THE CASE OF THE
FUN HOUSE
MYSTERY™

The Adventures of MARY-KATE & ASHLEY™

THE CASE OF THE FUN HOUSE MYSTERY™

A novelization by Nancy E. Krulik

WILL SOLVE ANY CRIME BY DINNER TIME™

DUALSTAR PUBLICATIONS PARACHUTE PRESS, INC.

SCHOLASTIC INC.

New York   Toronto   London   Auckland   Sydney

DUALSTAR PUBLICATIONS   PARACHUTE PRESS, INC.

Dualstar Publications
c/o 10100 Santa Monica Blvd.
Suite 2200
Los Angeles, CA 90067

Parachute Press, Inc.
156 Fifth Avenue
Suite 325
New York, NY 10010

Published by Scholastic Inc.

With special thanks to Robert Thorne and Harold Weitzberg.

Printed in the U.S.A.
June 1996
ISBN: 0-590-86231-6
D E F G H I J

Ready for Adventure?

It was the best of times. It was the worst of times. Actually it was bedtime when our great-grandmother would read us stories of mystery and suspense. It was then that we decided to be detectives.

The story you are about to read is one of the cases from the files of the Olsen and Olsen Mystery Agency. We call it *The Case Of The Fun House Mystery.*

Fun Houses are supposed to be filled with surprises. But the Fun House at the Tons of Fun Amusement Park had a very *scary* surprise inside. And we had to find out exactly what it was!

Who wanted to go near a not-so-fun Fun House? We did. We *had* to. It was our job to solve this mystery. After all, we always live up to our motto: Will Solve Any Crime By Dinner Time!

Chapter 1

RRRRGGHHH!

"What was that?" I wondered. I jumped to my feet and turned around. Right behind me was a very scary-looking creature. A creature with a huge, pointy nose, sharp white fangs, and little squinty eyes. A monster!

RRRRGGHHH! The creature roared again.

"Nice try, Ashley," I said.

I knew this wasn't *really* a monster.

It was my twin sister, Ashley, wearing a silly Halloween mask. Ashley whipped off the mask.

"Mary-Kate! How did you know it was me?" she asked.

"Easy!" I told her. "I'd know your voice anywhere. I can spot a phony monster a mile away. And I had a hunch you'd try something like this."

"You did?" Ashley asked. "I thought I could fool you."

"But you know that I'm learning *everything* about monsters. No one could fool me!" I told her.

My name is Mary-Kate Olsen. My sister Ashley and I are the Trenchcoat Twins. What do we do? We solve crimes. We love mysteries. We're detectives.

Ashley and I both are nine years old. We both have long strawberry blond hair and big blue eyes. Some people can't tell us apart. But we really are *totally* different.

Ashley takes her time about everything. She thinks and thinks about every problem. And then she thinks some more. She studies every possible clue before she makes a move. Then, when she does move, it is very, very slowly.

Not me. I work on hunches. I always want to jump right in!

And right now, I am really into reading about monsters. That's because of our older brother, Trent. Trent is eleven. He's always trying to scare Ashley and me by telling us really scary monster stories.

Now I know that most of his stories aren't true. I already read about a dozen books on monsters this summer. But my new book is the best one yet. It's called *Everything You Ever Wanted to Know About Monsters But Were Afraid to Ask.*

Ashley picked up the book. "I bet you don't know *everything* about monsters," she said.

"Bet I do! Go ahead. Ask me a question," I told her.

"All right. What monster jumps higher

than a house?" Ashley asked.

Uh-oh. I hadn't read *anything* about jumping monsters. I grabbed my monster book back from Ashley and flipped it open.

"Hold on, hold on. I think there was something about jumping monsters in chapter six," I said.

I turned to chapter six.

Nothing.

In fact, there was nothing anywhere in the book about monsters that jumped.

"I give up. What monster jumps higher than a house?" I asked Ashley.

"All monsters can jump higher than a house," she answered. "Because *houses* can't jump!" She burst into giggles and collapsed onto the floor.

I groaned. "You tell the worst jokes!"

"You tell some pretty bad ones, too," Ashley said.

"Well, we wouldn't have time to sit

around telling jokes if we had a mystery to solve," I told her.

"You're right, Mary-Kate," Ashley answered. "We do need a mystery. But there's just one problem."

"What's the problem?" I asked Ashley.

"The problem is it's too hot to find a mystery," Ashley answered.

It was August, and it was really, really hot in California. And it was really, really hot inside our office.

The office of the Olsen and Olsen Mystery Agency is in the attic of our house. And there's no air conditioning in the attic.

I checked our trusty thermometer. It said it was about a gazillion degrees in the attic. *Whoa!*

I moved closer to the fan. All it did was blow around the hot air, but it was better than nothing.

"Hey—I just thought of a mystery we can

solve," I said to Ashley. "And it's a real hot one!"

Ashley looked at me as if I were crazy. "What 'hot' mystery?" she asked.

"How to keep cool!" I answered. "Or we could solve our *favorite* mystery," I added. "Finding out how long it takes for an ice cream sundae to disappear!"

CRASH!

Our supply cabinet suddenly toppled to the floor!

Ashley and I jumped to our feet. Our detective supplies were scattered all over the floor: our tape recorder, magnifying glass, camera, plastic bags, and rubber gloves. Even our fingerprinting kit.

"Oops," a small voice said.

"Lizzie!" Ashley and I shouted together.

Our little sister, Lizzie, stood behind the toppled cabinet. Lizzie is six years old. She has blue eyes and blond hair just like us.

"Sorry. I was just practicing snooping. I want to be a super-duper snooper like you guys," Lizzie said. "Can I play with you?"

"We're not playing. We're working," I told her.

"You don't look like you're working," Lizzie said. "You don't look like you're doing anything!"

"We *are* doing something. We're busy getting ready to work," Ashley told her.

"Where's Trent? He's supposed to be playing with you," I added.

Trent was in charge while our mom and dad were out of the house. They were at the hardware store. They promised to bring back more fans to cool off our office.

"Yeah, where is Trent?" Ashley asked.

Lizzie shrugged.

"Trent!" I yelled down the stairs. "Hurry! Come quick! Emergency!"

We heard Trent's footsteps racing up to

the attic. He burst into our office.

"What's wrong? What's the emergency?" he asked.

"Lizzie's bored," Ashley answered.

"So find something for her to do! I'm busy arranging my lizard collection," Trent said. He looked mad.

"Well, Ashley and I have detective work to do," I told him. "And that's way more important than your silly lizards!"

"You're in charge. *You* find something for Lizzie to do," I said.

Trent sneered at us. "Okay. Come on," he said. He took Lizzie by the hand.

"I'll take you back downstairs," he told her.

"Good!" Lizzie said. "I don't want to play with them anyway."

"Let's leave these detectives to do what they do best," Trent added. *"Nothing!"*

As he and Lizzie walked out the door

Ashley and I stuck out our tongues at him. Luckily he didn't see us.

I bent down and started to pick up our supplies off the floor. But it was too hot even to do that.

"Let's go swimming," I told Ashley. "It's too hot to work."

"Huh-uh," said Ashley. "We might miss a phone call from someone who needs our help."

I sighed. Maybe Ashley had a point. What would happen if we weren't home when someone needed help with a mystery?

"I guess you're right," I said. "We could stay here a little while longer."

Ashlely pulled a tiny book from the pocket of her shorts. It was her new *Detective Manual*. It was filled with lots of great ideas for solving mysteries. Our great-grandmother sent one to each of us at the beginning of the summer. She found the books in a special bookstore that only sells books about mysteries.

"I want to read my *Detective Manual* again," Ashley told me. "So I'll be really ready when the phone rings."

"You're wasting your time," I said. "It's too hot for mysteries. I have a hunch that phone is *never* going to ring."

Rrrinngg!

Oops!

My hunch was wrong.

Chapter 2

Ashley and I each picked up a phone. We have two phones on our desk. Mine is pink and Ashley's is blue.

We answered the call the same way we always do.

"Olsen and Olsen Mystery Agency. Will solve any crime by dinner time!"

"Hello?" a woman with a deep voice replied. "Who am I speaking to?"

"Ashley Olsen," Ashley said.

"And Mary-Kate Olsen," I added.

"Hello, darlings! This is Madame Zelda," the woman introduced herself. "I am calling from the Tons of Fun Amusement Park."

We heard some other voices talking in the background.

"Hey, what about me?" one voice shouted. "And me?" another voice added.

"My friends are here with me," Madame Zelda said. "Ferris Wheel Fred and Carousel Cal. Fred runs the Ferris wheel. Cal runs the carousel," she explained. "Say hello to the darlings, darlings," she told Fred and Cal.

"Hello, darlings," a high squeaky voice shouted into the phone. "This is Fred."

"Hello, darlings," a low, rumbling voice put in. "This is Cal."

"Hello, darlings," Ashley and I shouted back.

"Why are we shouting? Let's be calm about this," Madame Zelda said.

"Be calm about what?" I asked her.

"About the terrible thing that has happened," Madame Zelda answered.

"An awful, horrible thing," Fred's high

voice squeaked.

"An awful, horrible, terrible thing that we never expected," Cal's low voice rumbled.

"I, Madame Zelda, am a fortune-teller. I predict the future. But what happened today even I could not predict!" Madame Zelda sighed.

"What happened?" Ashley asked her.

"I'm almost afraid to tell you. But since we are all friends now, I will." Madame Zelda took a deep breath. "We have a mystery in our Fun House!"

Yes!

Ashley and I slapped a high five.

"We were waiting for a mystery to solve," Ashley told her.

"She's right," I said. "But hold on, Madame Zelda," I told her. "I need a few detective supplies."

I took out my detective notebook and a pen. Our great-grandma gave me the notebook. I use it to write down clues. A good detective always takes careful notes. And lots of them. Because you never know which information will turn out to be the most important.

"Tell us everything," Ashley said when I was ready.

"Well, Fred, Cal, and I have had a positively horrible day," Madame Zelda began. "We couldn't finish setting up the Fun House."

"The Fun House is the newest, scariest attraction in the amusement park," Cal explained.

"We call it the Creepy Crawly Fun House," Fred added.

"Because it's the creepiest, crawliest Fun House ever!" Madame Zelda told us.

"And we've seen some very creepy fun houses," Fred added.

"We fixed it up with scary sounds, gruesome ghosts, and slippery spiderwebs," Madame Zelda continued. "It is definitely not for nervous types."

"Well, that sounds like a lot of fun," I said. "But there's nothing mysterious about a Fun House."

"Oh, yes, there is!" Fred shouted. "There's something living in this Fun House."

Ashley frowned. "Who'd want to live in your Fun House?" she asked.

"No one. I mean, it's not a *someone* living in the Fun House. It's a some*thing*," Madame Zelda told us.

"Something with a big appetite!" Cal added.

"That's for sure," Fred agreed. "Because this something stole my lunch. A huge peanut butter and banana sandwich!"

Ashley and I looked at each other in excitement. This was starting to sound spooky. *And* mysterious!

"Has anyone seen this something?" I asked. I got ready to write down the answer.

"No one's seen it," Fred said.

"But they've *heard* it," Cal added.

"Yes, that's the worst of it, darlings," Madame Zelda said. "This some*thing* makes a terrible sound."

"A sound that makes your blood freeze," Cal added.

"A sound that makes your hair stand on end," Fred said.

I took notes as quickly as I could. Then I showed them to Ashley.

MYSTERY: Some*thing* living in the Creepy Crawly Fun House.

CLUES: Big appetite.

Steals peanut butter and banana sandwiches.

Makes terrible sound that makes blood freeze and hair stand on end.

Ashley and I looked at each other again.

"Are you thinking what I'm thinking?" I asked her. Ashley nodded.

I took a deep breath.

"Madame Zelda, we think we know what your problem is," I said. "And you're *not* going to like it!"

Chapter 3

"There's a *monster* in your Fun House!" Ashley and I said together.

Madame Zelda gasped.

"A monster!" we heard Fred and Cal shout.

"Oh, dear, I hope we don't have a monster," Madame Zelda said. "People only like *pretend* monsters. They're tons of fun. But nobody likes a Fun House that has a *real* monster living in it!"

"Well, there might be another explanation," Ashley told them. "But a monster sounds logical to me."

"What kind of a monster is it?" Fred asked.

"Is it very dangerous?" Cal asked.

"How do we get rid of it?" Madame Zelda asked.

"We don't know—yet. But don't worry," I told them. "The Trenchcoat Twins are on the case! And we'll get to the bottom of this before you can say 'Tons of Fun'!"

Ashley and I hung up the phone and got right to work.

Ashley checked the map to figure out the shortest way to get to the Tons of Fun Amusement Park.

I packed up everything we would need to investigate this case. Our camera, our tape recorder, and of course, my trusty notebook. I also packed plenty of plastic bags to hold any clues and evidence we found.

"Ready, Detective Olsen?" I asked.

"Ready, Detective Olsen," Ashley answered.

Ashley slipped on her hot-pink backpack.

I slipped on my blue backpack. We each put on our favorite sunglasses.

Then we hurried downstairs and out of the house. We grabbed our bicycle helmets and wheeled our bikes into the driveway.

"Where's Clue?" I asked.

Did I mention that we have a silent partner? She's our dog, Clue. Clue is a brown and white Basset hound with floppy ears and a big wet nose—just perfect for sniffing out clues. We take her wherever we go.

"Here, Clue! Here, girl!" Ashley called.

Clue ran out from under a big shady tree.

"Good dog," Ashley said. She patted Clue's head.

"We've got a case to solve. Want to help?" I asked.

"Woof!" Clue barked.

Ashley and I lifted Clue into my bicycle basket. We were ready to roll!

"Hey! Where are you two going?" Trent's

voice called down from his open bedroom window.

Major problem!

"Uh, well, umm…" Ashley stuttered.

"We were just checking the air in our bicycle tires," I told him.

"Quick thinking!" Ashley whispered to me.

"Well, you better not be sneaking off without asking my permission," Trent shouted. "Because *I'm* in charge! And I say you're not going anywhere!"

Trent slammed his window shut.

"Now what are we going to do? We have to help Madame Zelda," Ashley said.

I thought hard for a few minutes.

"I have the perfect plan!" I said. I whispered my plan in Ashley's ear.

Ashley grinned. "Let's do it!" she said.

Ashley and I hurried back into the house. We stopped in our room. Then we walked down the hall to Lizzie's room. Lizzie was sitting at her little plastic table, coloring with crayons.

"Time for phase one of our plan," Ashley whispered. We stepped into Lizzie's room.

I gave Lizzie my brightest smile. "Lizzie, would you like to play with our brand-new watercolor paints?"

Lizzie looked amazed. Ashley and I hardly ever let her touch our stuff.

"Sure!" she exclaimed.

I gave Lizzie the paints, a paintbrush, and a big pan of water. I did not give her a smock to cover her clothes or a cloth to cover the carpet.

Lizzie started to paint. She splashed bright colors all over the paper—and all over everything else, too.

"Time for phase two," Ashley whispered to me.

We walked into Trent's room.

"Hey, Trent," I said. "I think you have a problem. Lizzie's painting—and you'd better have a look!"

Trent sprang off his bed. "Oh, man," he moaned.

Trent raced into Lizzie's room. His mouth dropped open. There was red paint all over the carpet. There was blue paint on the table and chairs. There was yellow paint on the walls. And there was green paint all over Lizzie.

"Lizzie! This will take hours to clean up!" Trent shouted. He grabbed the paints away from Lizzie and hurried down the hall to find sponges and paper towels.

"Come on, Ashley," I whispered. "Time for us to get going—before Trent comes back!"

We hurried back outside. Clue was very glad to see us. She wagged her tail like crazy. Ashley and I hopped on our bikes and headed for the Tons of Fun Amusement Park.

"Pedal fast, Ashley," I said.

"I'm pedalling as fast as I can," she replied.

"Okay, okay," I said. "Just remember, we have to solve this crime by dinner time!"

Chapter 4

"Helloooo, darlings!"

Madame Zelda was waiting for us at the gate of the Tons of Fun Amusement Park. She was dressed in bright colors from head to toe. An orange scarf was tied around her long black hair. She wore a long skirt made of red, orange, and purple patches in all shapes and sizes. And around her shoulders she wore a bright red shawl with gold stars all over it.

"You must be Madame Zelda," I said.

"I am, darlings! And this is Ferris Wheel Fred." Madame Zelda pointed to a tall, thin man standing next to her. Fred was wearing a bright red shirt under a tan vest. A big hat perched on his head.

"And this is Carousel Cal," she added. A short, plump man on her other side bowed. Cal wore a green shirt under his brown vest. He lifted his gray hat to say hello.

Ashley and I parked our bikes. We lifted Clue out of her basket.

"Woof!" Clue barked. She sniffed at Madame Zelda and licked her hand. Then she sniffed at Fred and Cal.

"Yikes!" Fred leaped onto Cal's shoulders. "A monster!" he shouted.

Ashley and I smiled at each other.

"Clue's not a monster," Ashley told Fred. "She's our dog. Clue's here to help us solve the mystery."

"Oh," Fred said. He bent down to pet Clue.

Madame Zelda reached over and pinched our cheeks. "You two are so adorable!" she said. "And twins yet!"

"We might be adorable. But we're serious detectives. And it's time to get down to business," Ashley said.

I looked all around me. "So this is the Tons of Fun Amusement Park?"

Fred and Cal were shocked. "You mean you've never been here before?" Fred asked.

"Let's give them the tour!" Cal said.

Madame Zelda agreed. "A very special tour! The V.I.T. tour!"

"Don't you mean V.I.P.? For Very Important Persons?" I asked.

"V.I.T. For Very Important Twins!" Madame Zelda replied.

"Great! Because I can't wait to go on all the rides," I said.

Madame Zelda led us through the amusement park.

We stopped at a cart piled high with delicious food.

"What'll you have, darlings?" Madame Zelda asked us. "How about some sweet and sticky cotton candy? Or you might want to try a stack of steaming hot dogs."

"Cotton candy for me," Ashley said.

"I'll have a hot dog," I said.

We gobbled our food as Madame Zelda led us to the arcade of games.

"KNOCK DOWN THE DUCKS AND WIN A PRIZE!" read one sign. "TOSS THE RING INTO THE BARREL! EVERYONE'S A WINNER!" said another sign.

Ashley and I took turns at both games. I knocked down three ducks in a row. Ashley threw rings in a giant barrel. We won an armful of stuffed animals as prizes. *Cool!*

But the best part of our tour was the rides. The Ferris wheel was the tallest we had ever seen.

The Snap-the-Whip roller coaster zoomed up and up and up—and then raced way back down.

The Tilt-A-Whirl flew around in circles.

"Let's try the Tilt-A-Whirl," I said.

"Hop right on," Fred said.

Ashley and I jumped into a cart that lifted and spun around like crazy. I thought it was tons of fun.

Ashley looked a little green. "I'm dizzy," she complained.

"What ride will you try next, darlings?" Madame Zelda asked.

"No ride," Ashley said.

"But Ashley, we can pick any ride we want," I pointed out. "We have the whole place to ourselves."

"That's exactly what's wrong," Ashley told me. "Didn't you notice? No one else is on the rides."

I looked all around the park. Ashley was right. The Tons of Fun Amusement Park *was* completely empty! I shivered. This was really weird.

"Uh, maybe we won't go on any more rides. An empty amusement park is kind of creepy," I said.

"Yeah. Where is everyone?" Ashley asked.

Madame Zelda looked as if she were going to cry.

"No one will come to the park. Not since the word got out that something creepy is living in the Fun House," she told us.

"No one comes to try the rides. Or play the games. Or eat the food!" Fred added.

"If you can't solve this mystery, we'll have to close the park forever!" Madame Zelda sighed. Tears came to her eyes.

"Then we'd better take a look at the Fun House right away," I said.

"Good idea, darlings," Madame Zelda said. She led us across the park.

"Here it is! This is where all the trouble started." Madame Zelda pointed to a sign that said THE CREEPY CRAWLY FUN HOUSE.

Ashley and I stared at the Fun House. The entrance looked like a giant clown's head. The clown's big red mouth hung wide open. To get into the Fun House you walked right into the mouth!

"This is definitely creepy crawly," I said, staring into the big red mouth. No way was I going in there!

"Definitely creepy," Ashley agreed. "Maybe we should look for a few more clues out here. Like what's all that?" Ashley pointed to a pile of empty crates that were stacked up close to the Fun House.

"Woof!" Clue barked. She raced over and began sniffing the crates. Her tail wagged back and forth in excitement.

Ashley and I followed her.

"Those are just empty boxes," Madame Zelda said, shrugging.

I pulled out my notebook. "Well, they could be an important clue," I said. I wrote about the boxes in my notebook.

CLUE: Empty boxes next to Clown Head.

"What was in these boxes?" Ashley asked.

"Very scary things," Madame Zelda answered. "We used them to decorate the Fun House."

Fred pointed to a crate with the words HAIRY SPIDERS written across the lid. "We hung up hundreds and hundreds of really creepy, crawly plastic spiders in the Fun House," he explained.

"And spooky skeletons and slimy snakes," Cal added.

"We just love to decorate," Madame Zelda said.

"What was in *that* box?" Ashley asked. She pointed to a crate that was hidden behind the others. "I can only see the letter P on the lid," she said.

I looked up from my detective's notebook.

Fred moved a few crates out of the way. He lifted up the crate with the letter P on it. Now we could see the words written on the lid.

"Pongo pygmaeus," Fred read.

"Pongo pyga-what-us?" I asked.

"Pongo pygmaeus," Fred read again.

"What's that?" Ashley asked.

Fred shrugged. Cal shrugged.

"Never heard of it," Madame Zelda replied.

Ashley examined the crate with her magnifying glass. "There's a label on this crate. The label tells you where the crate is going. And this crate going to a country called Borneo," she said.

More clues!

I wrote in my notebook.

OTHER CLUES: Empty crate is marked Pongo pygmaeus. Crate being sent to Borneo.

"Well, I don't think there are any more

clues around here," Ashley said.

"That means only one thing." I said. I took a deep breath. Ashley did too.

"It's time to find the monster," we said together.

We're Mary-Kate and Ashley—the Trenchcoat Twins. There we were at home—waiting for someone to call with a new mystery to solve!

In the meantime, our biggest mystery was trying to figure out why summer was so hot!

At last! We got a call from Cal, Madame Zelda, and Fred—the owners of the Tons of Fun Amusement Park.

Oh, no! Something was hiding in their Fun House. And it was scaring away all of the customers.

Tons of Fun was very cool! Ashley and I ate lots of cotton candy and won stuffed animals and prizes.

Madame Zelda showed us her crystal ball.

Fred took us on a scary ride.

Then we checked out the not-so-fun Fun House. What were those creepy noises? Was there a monster inside?

We visited Dr. Peabody. He is a monster expert.

Dr. Peabody knows everything about monsters—
even how their brains work!

We solved the mystery. The monster was not a monster—it was an orangutan!

Madame Zelda, Fred, and Cal thanked us and gave us free passes to the Tons of Fun Amusement Park.

How did the orangutan end up at the Tons of Fun Amusement Park in the first place? We figured it out—can you?

Chapter 5

Clue followed us up to the Fun House door. She sniffed. Then she let out a frightened yelp.

"What's wrong with her?" Madame Zelda asked.

ROOOAAAR!

Cal and Fred jumped and hid in back of Madame Zelda's big skirt.

"That's it!" Cal said.

"That's the monster!" Fred said.

ROOOAAAR!

The terrible sound came from deep inside the Fun House.

Gulp. The monster sounded really mad!

"Go ahead, Ashley. You first." I pushed my sister toward the Fun House door.

"Me? Why do I have to go first?" she asked.

"Because you're the oldest," I answered.

"Only by two minutes," Ashley said.

"Right. And I'll be only two minutes behind you," I said.

"No way!" Ashley shook her head.

"You're not afraid, are you, darlings?" Madame Zelda asked. She looked worried.

Ashley and I straightened our shoulders.

"The Trenchcoat Twins? Afraid?" I asked.

"Only a little bit," Ashley said.

"But don't worry," I added. "After all, I'm practically an expert on monsters!"

I took Ashley's hand. She squeezed my fingers. Hard.

We walked into the clown's mouth together. Clue followed close behind us. We entered a big, square room.

It was dark. Very dark. There was just enough light to see the creepy creatures that stood along the walls.

We walked past a giant rubber bat. We jumped back as its wings started flapping up and down. Clue howled.

"Whoa!" I said. "I hate bats!"

Ashley squeezed my arm. "Remember— it's just a rubber bat. Cal and Fred put it in here," she said.

Ashley turned to go in the other direction. A hand reached out to grab her. A skeleton's hand!

"Yikes!" Ashley yelled.

"Remember—it's only a plastic skeleton," I said.

We both took another step. Something bright flashed before our eyes.

"Yikes!" I exclaimed.

"Watch out!" Ashley said.

We had almost walked into a statue of a

pirate. A pirate waving a huge, shiny sword over his head.

"Woof! Woof!" Clue barked.

"It's okay, Clue," I told her. "This stuff can't really hurt us. It's all fake." My voice was shaking.

"Right. It all came out of a crate," Ashley added. Her voice was shaking, too.

Whap!

Something plopped down from the ceiling. It landed on my head.

"Aaaah!" I screamed.

"Mary-Kate! Are you okay?" Ashley asked.

I pulled the thing off my head and dropped it on the floor. "I'm fine. It's only a rubber spider," I said.

"What's so fun about this Fun House anyway?" Ashley asked.

"Beats me," I answered. "Let's find the monster and get out of here!"

We stepped out of the big room. We

found ourselves in front of a long, dark tunnel. The tunnel led into the rest of the Fun House.

Ashley sniffed the air in the tunnel. "Whew! What is that awful smell?" she asked.

"I don't know. But it reminds me of the zoo!" I said.

"I don't like this tunnel. Let's hurry and get out of here." Ashley took a step. We both heard a loud squishing sound.

We glanced down. Ashley had stepped in something brown and mushy.

"Yuck!" Ashley said.

I reached into our bag of supplies and pulled out a pooper-scooper. (A good detective never leaves home without a pooper-scooper!) I scooped up some of the mushy brown stuff and slid it into a plastic bag.

"What is it?" Ashley asked.

"Some kind of monster mush." I sniffed. "Hmmmm. I think I've smelled *this* before too," I said. I took another sniff.

"I'm not very happy in here," Ashley told me.

"Relax, Ashley," I said.

"I can't relax. Because there's one problem," Ashley said. "Where there's monster mush, there's usually…"

ROOOOAAAARRRR!

"A MONSTER!" Ashley finished.

Clue raised her head and howled. "Woof!" she barked. Then she ran into the tunnel—right toward the monster!

"Clue, wait!" I yelled.

"There's a monster down there!" Ashley shouted.

I ran into the tunnel after Clue. I had to bring her back!

"Mary-Kate! Wait!" Ashley yelled.

I kept running. Suddenly something hairy brushed against my bare arm. Something very *big* and hairy.

"Clue?" I asked. My voice came out in a whisper.

A paw brushed against my face. A very *large* paw.

"Eeeeeaahh!" I screamed.

Chapter 6

I didn't know what was on the other end of that paw. But it *definitely* wasn't Clue!

I ran back through the tunnel. Ashley was pacing the floor.

"There you are!" she said. "What happened?" she asked.

"I found the monster! It attacked me!" I shouted.

"Wow!" Ashley took a deep breath. "We'd better go back and get a picture of it," she said.

I stared at her. "Ashley, it attacked me. Do you really think we should go back in there?" I asked.

"I don't *want* to," Ashley said. "But we have to take some pictures. We need evidence that there really *is* a monster in the Fun House."

How could she be so logical at a time like this?

I sighed. I reached into my backpack and pulled out the camera. "Okay," I said. "Let's go."

We both ran back into the tunnel. I aimed the camera at the place where the monster grabbed me.

ROOOAAAR!

I pushed the button to take a picture. A bright light flashed in my eyes.

"Uh, Mary-Kate—you just took a picture of your own face!" Ashley said.

Ooops! The camera was pointed the wrong way.

"Sorry," I said.

"There's no time for sorry!" Ashley told

me. "Get a picture of that monster before he runs away!"

"Why would he run away?" I asked.

"Because the flash from the camera probably scared him," Ashley said.

ROOOAAAR!! The monster was coming closer!

"Uh, Ashley—I don't think the monster is scared. I think he's *mad*. So can we go now?" I asked.

"Not yet," Ashley said. She was bent over her backpack.

"What are you doing?" I asked.

"Making a tape recording of the monster's roar," Ashley said.

"Good. Can we can get out of here now?" I asked.

"Not yet. You need to take more photos," Ashley said.

I pointed the camera down the tunnel again. I snapped picture after picture. With each flash of light I could see a part of the monster.

I saw a red hairy hand. I saw huge, hairy feet. I saw tiny, gleaming eyes. I saw pointy, sharp-looking teeth.

Gulp. This was one scary-looking monster!

"Woof!" Suddenly Clue raced between my legs. She headed away from the monster. She ran straight for the Fun House door.

"Ashley, maybe Clue is on to something. Like maybe it really is time to get out of here?" I said.

ROOOAAAR!!!

"Uh—Ashley," I said. "I think we should go. And *fast*!"

A huge hairy arm slashed through the air. It swiped at our tape recorder.

"Uh—maybe you're right," Ashley said. She picked up the tape recorder.

I turned and ran. And ran. Then I realized that Ashley wasn't behind me.

"Ashley? Where are you?" I called.

Ashley's voice called back from the Fun House.

"Help! Help!" she cried. "It's got me!"

Chapter 7

The monster had Ashley. I had no time to be scared. No time to think. I just had to help my sister.

"Don't worry! I'll save you!" I yelled.

I took a deep breath. Then I ran back inside the Fun House. Clue was right behind me. I could see Ashley at the opening of the tunnel. I could hear her scream.

"Let me go!" she yelled.

I stared straight ahead as I ran. In the darkness, I could see the monster's hairy paw holding on to Ashley's sneaker!

I rushed up to Ashley and grabbed her arm. "Let her go!" I screamed at the monster.

I tugged on Ashley's arm with all my strength. The monster tugged on Ashley's foot. We were having an Ashley tug-of-war!

"Ouch! That hurts," Ashley cried.

"Woof! Woof!" Clue leaped into the air. She yelped and barked.

I saw the hairy paw let go of Ashley's sneaker. Ashley was free!

Ashley, Clue, and I raced out of the Fun House. We ran straight to Madame Zelda's fortune-telling tent.

"It's definitely a monster!" I told Madame Zelda.

"You are such good detectives, darlings!" Madame Zelda said. "Your parents must be *soooo* proud," she added. She reached out and pinched our cheeks.

"Thanks," we mumbled.

"What kind of monster is it?" Fred asked.

"Well, we still can't answer that question," Ashley said.

"But we do have a lot more clues," I told all of them.

"Like this tape recording of the monster's roar," Ashley added.

She pulled out our tape recorder and played back the sound of the monster howling. Cal and Fred dove under the table. They were really scared of that monster!

"And we have these photographs," I added. I spread the pictures across the table.

"Oooh!" said Fred. He stared at the photos of the monster's pointy teeth.

"Aaaah!" added Cal. He stared at the photos of the monster's gleaming eyes.

"That is one red hairy monster!" said Madame Zelda. She stared at the photos of the monster's huge feet.

"And that's not all," I told them. I took out the bag of mush. "We also have a bag full of monster mush!"

"Yuck!" Fred exclaimed.

"That mush looks totally disgusting," Cal added.

"I'm glad that we know more about the monster. But we still don't know how to get rid of it," Madame Zelda pointed out.

"But we *do* know someone who can help us," I said.

"And with all these clues, he'll probably know just what kind of monster you have," Ashley said.

"Yes. Because he knows even more about monsters than I do," I added.

"But who is this wonderful person?" Madame Zelda asked.

"Dr. Percival Peabody, Professor of Monstrology," I answered.

"Can you talk to this Dr. Peabody soon?" Madame Zelda asked.

"We're on our way right now!" I said.

"And don't worry. We always solve our crimes by dinner time!" Ashley added.

Ashley and I gathered all our clues. We packed up our equipment and loaded Clue back into my bicycle basket.

We jumped on our bikes and headed straight for State College. We reached Dr. Peabody's office in record time. Luckily he was there. He was happy to see us.

"Mary-Kate! Ashley! My favorite twin detectives! Come in," he said.

"We need your help, Dr. Peabody," I told him.

"We have to get rid of a monster in the Fun House," Ashley added.

We dumped our clues onto Dr. Peabody's desk.

"Hmmmm." He poked at the monster mush. "Yuck. This certainly looks disgusting," he told us.

He studied the photographs. "Definitely frightening," he told us.

He listened to the tape recording of the

monster's roar. "Absolutely monstrous!" he said.

He read through all our notes.

Dr. Peabody scratched his head.

He pulled out one of his big, fat monster books. "Pongo pygmaeus...Pongo pygmaeus," he said. He read quickly through the book.

"There's no Pongo pygmaeus anywhere in here! Still, I have lots of books. If you give me a few days, I'm sure I'll be able to identify the monster for you."

"A few days?" I said.

"A few days?" Ashley repeated.

Clue lay down on the floor. She covered her eyes with her paws and whimpered.

"We don't have a few days," I said.

"We have to live up to our motto: Will solve any crime by dinner time," Ashley told Dr. Peabody.

He sighed. "I'm very sorry," he said.

"So are we," I told him.

Ashley and I packed up our things and went outside.

"What do we do now?" I wondered. "We can't solve the crime by dinner time!"

"We have no choice," Ashley said. "We have to go back to the amusement park. We have to tell Madame Zelda that we can't solve her mystery. Not today, anyway."

We climbed back on our bikes. I felt terrible. Ashley felt terrible. Even Clue looked really unhappy.

We rode along in silence. We passed the movie theater. We passed the tennis courts. We passed the zoo.

"Mary-Kate! Stop!" Ashley cried out.

I put on my brakes. "What is it?" I asked.

"Didn't you say that the smell in the Fun House reminded you of the zoo?" Ashley asked.

"So?" I stared at her.

"So maybe we'll find a really important clue in here," Ashley said.

I felt a burst of excitement.

Yes!

I had a hunch that the answer to the mystery was right under our noses—in the zoo!

Chapter 8

I jumped off my bike and ran into the zoo.

"Wait, Mary-Kate! I need your help," Ashley yelled.

I ran back to Ashley and helped her lift Clue out of the bicycle basket. I put Clue on her leash.

"Okay, let's go in," I said.

"Hang on, Mary-Kate. Check your notes. Do we know what we're looking for?"

I whipped out my trusty detective's notebook.

"We're looking for a red hairy monster. A monster with a very loud roar. A monster who likes peanut butter and banana sandwiches. A monster who answers to the name Pongo pygmaeus."

We hurried into the zoo. We heard a loud roar!

Ashley and I ran up to a metal fence. Inside was a special area for the bears.

Roooar!

"Could the monster be a bear?" I asked Ashley.

Just then the animal trainer came by with a bucket of bear food. He threw the food to the hungry bears.

"Bears don't eat bananas and peanut butter," Ashley pointed out.

Clue raised her nose in the air and sniffed. "Woof!" she barked.

"Right, Clue," I told her. "This isn't the smell that was in the Fun House."

Ashley nodded. "And these bears have brown fur. Our monster has red fur. We'd better keep looking."

Ashley and I moved on. We walked past the lion's den. The lion let out a mighty roar. Clue leaped into my arms. She'd never heard a cat sound like *that* before!

Ashley played back the roar on our tape recorder.

"This roar is different. And lions have paws, not hands. And they aren't red *or* very hairy. So our monster can't be a lion," I said.

Clue raised her head and sniffed again. "Woof! Woof!" she barked and started to run.

"Follow that dog!" I yelled.

Clue ran straight to the monkey house. She raised her head and howled—exactly the way she did in the Fun House!

"You're right, Clue," I said. "That smell is awfully familiar!"

"And look—bananas!" Ashley exclaimed.

Bananas grew on tall trees all around the monkey house. More bananas lay scattered on the ground.

ROOOAAAR!

"Listen to that!" I said.

Ashley played back the roar on our tape recorder.

"Yes! It's the same roar!" she said.

We hurried closer. "Ashley! Look at that sign!"

I grabbed her arm and pointed to the wall of the monkey house. Ashley read the sign.

"Yes!" she shouted.

We slapped a high five.

"All right!" I yelled. "Our mystery is solved!"

Chapter 9

"Now we know everything about the monster! I can't wait to tell Madame Zelda!" I said.

Ashley, Clue, and I raced out of the zoo. We hopped on our bikes. We pedalled as fast as we could.

In no time we were back at the Tons of Fun Amusement Park. We hurried to the Creepy Crawly Fun House.

ROOOAAAR!

Pongo Pygmaeus roared as loud as ever.

Cal and Fred were still hiding behind Madame Zelda. Madame Zelda was trying to put a lock on the door of the Fun House.

"It's okay, guys. You don't have to be scared anymore," Ashley told Cal and Fred.

"And you don't need to put a lock on the door, Madame Zelda," I added.

"I don't?" Madame Zelda asked.

"No. Because Pongo Pygmaeus is *not* a monster."

"Then what is he, darlings?" asked Madame Zelda.

"He's a big monkey! An *orangutan!*" I answered. "A lost, frightened orangutan."

Madame Zelda looked amazed.

"We figured it all out at the zoo. We smelled the same smell that was in the Fun House," I said. "We followed our noses—like good detectives."

"They led us to the monkey area—and to Pongo pygmaeus," Ashley added.

"Pongo pygmaeus is the scientific name for an orangutan," I explained. "We read it on a sign at the zoo."

"That's why our wonderful friend Dr. Peabody couldn't find Pongo pygmaeus listed in his monster book," Ashley said. "Because an orangutan *isn't* a monster."

"And we figured out that the monster mush is really squished bananas," Ashley said. "Monkeys love bananas!"

"But how did he get here?" Cal asked.

"He must have been shipped here by mistake," I said.

"Darlings, you are amazing detectives," Madame Zelda told us. She pinched our cheeks.

"Fred, Cal, and I are so grateful! We are giving your whole family a free pass to the Tons of Fun Amusement Park. Come back anytime!" Madame Zelda said.

"Thanks!" Ashley and I said together.

"But what are we going to do with the orangutan?" Fred asked.

"Why don't you send him back to

Borneo?" I said.

"That's where orangutans come from," Ashley added. "It said so on the sign at the zoo."

"I guess he was trying to get home all along," I said. "I bet he misses his family."

Madame Zelda smiled. "You're right, darlings! He'll soon be with his family again. But first, let's give our friend some food!"

Madame Zelda left. She came back holding a bunch of ripe bananas. She opened the Fun House door.

"Come and get it!" Madame Zelda called. "Dinner time!"

Uh-oh!

Ashley and I looked at each other.

"Dinner time! Well, we solved the crime on time," I said.

"Yeah, but now we have a new problem," Ashley added. "We're late for dinner with our family!"

Chapter 10

Ashley and I raced home as fast as we could. We threw down our bikes. We ran into the kitchen, huffing and puffing. Clue was right behind us. We were fast, but not fast enough. Our whole family was sitting at the table.

"You guys missed dinner! You're really in trouble!" Trent said. He grinned.

"You even missed dessert!" Lizzie added. She seemed surprised.

Mom had that look on her face—the look she gets when she doesn't know if she's angry or happy to see us.

"Where have you been?" she asked.

"You're very late," Dad said.

"Guilty," I said.

"With an explanation," Ashley added.

"You see, there was a monster in a Fun House," I began.

"Well, it wasn't really a monster," Ashley told them.

"But Madame Zelda thought it was," I said.

"And so did Fred and Cal," Ashley added.

"Hold on, you two," Dad said. "Start from the beginning. And tell us *everything*."

So we did. We told them how the orangutan was shipped to the Fun House by mistake. And how everyone thought he was a monster and they were too scared to go in the amusement park. And how we figured out that he *wasn't* a monster. And how it was our idea to send him home to Borneo.

"So Madame Zelda is happy. Fred and Cal are happy. And soon the orangutan will be happy, too!" Ashley said.

"Right. Everyone is happy," I added.

"Not so fast. *I'm* not happy," Mom said. "It took Trent hours to clean Lizzie's carpet. And Lizzie had to take two baths to wash off all that paint."

Oops! I'd forgotten about that.

"You girls owe your brother an apology. You left the house without his permission," Mom added.

"And to show him how sorry you are, you'll do his chores for a week," Dad added.

Ashley and I groaned. "Okay," we both said.

"Hooray!" Trent shouted.

Now Mom and Dad and Trent were happy.

"There's some more good news," I told everyone. "We're all invited to the Tons of Fun Amusement Park anytime we like."

"And for free!" Ashley added.

Lizzie's eyes lit up with excitement. Now she was happy, too.

Trent cheered. "Can we go there tomorrow?" he asked Mom and Dad.

"Sure. As soon as all your sisters' chores are done," Mom answered.

Yes! Ashley and I slapped a high five.

"Great!" I said. "Because I can't wait to *monkey around* in that Fun House!"

Now *everyone* was happy!

Hi—from both of us!

Solving the mystery in a super-spooky amusement park was tough work. Our scariest case yet! Still, Ashley and I had a monstrously good time!

So good that we couldn't wait for our next high-flying adventure. We never dreamed what kind of thrills and chills were waiting for us. Because this time, the clues were really out of this world!

Don't waste another minute. Blast off to adventure with us as you read all about *The Case Of The U.S. Space Camp Mission*. And, in the meantime, if you have any questions, you can write us at:

MARY-KATE + ASHLEY'S FUN CLUB™
859 HOLLYWOOD WAY, SUITE 412
BURBANK, CA 91505

We would love to hear from you!

*Love
Mary-Kate and Ashley*

The Adventures of MARY-KATE & ASHLEY™

A brand-new book series starring the Olsen Twins!
Based on their best-selling detective home video series.

Join the Trenchcoat Twins™—Mary-Kate and Ashley—as
they find mystery, adventure and fun!

Book One:
The Case Of The Sea World® Adventure™
Book Two:
The Case Of The Mystery Cruise™
Book Three:
The Case Of The Fun House Mystery™
Book Four:
The Case Of The U.S. Space Camp® Mission™
Book Five:
The Case Of The Christmas Caper™
(coming December 1996)
And Super Special #1:
from their other best-selling home video series
You're Invited To Mary-Kate & Ashley's™
Sleepover Party™
*A book with a special Mary-Kate & Ashley locket
just for you!*
(coming October 1996)

**Look for these great books all year long from Dualstar Publications and
Parachute Press, Inc., published by *Scholastic*.**

It doesn't matter if you live around the corner...
or around the world...
If you are a fan of Mary-Kate and Ashley Olsen,
you should be a member of

MARY-KATE + ASHLEY'S FUN CLUB™

Here's what you get:
Our Funzine™
An autographed color photo
Two black & white individual photos
A full size color poster
An official **Fun Club**™ membership card
A **Fun Club**™ school folder
Two special **Fun Club**™ surprises
A holiday card
Fun Club™ collectibles catalog
Plus a **Fun Club**™ box to keep everything in

To join Mary-Kate + Ashley's Fun Club™, fill out the form
below and send it along with

U.S. Residents – $17.00
Canadian Residents – $22 U.S. Funds
International Residents – $27 U.S. Funds

**MARY-KATE + ASHLEY'S FUN CLUB™
859 HOLLYWOOD WAY, SUITE 275
BURBANK, CA 91505**

NAME:_____

ADDRESS:_____

CITY:_____STATE:_____ZIP:_____

PHONE: (____) _____BIRTHDATE:_____

The Adventures of MARY-KATE & ASHLEY ™
THE VIDEOS

Look for these best-selling detective home video episodes!
Starring the Trenchcoat Twins™, your favorite stars,
Mary-Kate & Ashley Olsen!

The Case Of The Mystery Cruise™	**53302-3**
The Case Of The Logical i Ranch™	**53303-3**
The Case Of The Sea World® Adventure™	**53301-3**
The Case Of Thorn Mansion™	**53300-3**
The Case Of The Fun House Mystery™	**53306-3**
The Case Of The Christmas Caper™	**53305-3**
The Case Of The U.S. Space Camp® Mission™	**53320-3**
The Case Of The Shark Encounter™	**53321-3**

And also available:

Mary-Kate & Ashley Olsen: Our First Video™	**53304-3**
You're Invited To Mary-Kate & Ashley's™ *Sleepover Party*™	**53307-3**

DUALSTAR VIDEO

WILL SOLVE ANY CRIME • BY DINNER TIME ™

~ The Adventures of ~
MARY-KATE & ASHLEY ™
LIFTOFF WITH THE TRENCHCOAT TWINS™ U.S. SPACE CAMP® SWEEPSTAKES

YOU CAN WIN A PARENT/CHILD WEEKEND AT U.S. SPACE CAMP®, SEE A NASA SHUTTLE LAUNCH*, AND MEET THE OLSEN TWINS.

Complete this entry form and send to:
Liftoff With the Trenchcoat Twins
C/O Scholastic Trade Marketing Dept.
P.O. Box 7500
Jefferson City, MO 65102-7500

Name_____
(please print)

Address_____

City_____ State_____ Zip_____

Phone Number (_____) _____

DUALSTAR VIDEO

*subject to availability
No purchase necessary to enter. Sweepstakes entries must
be received by 10/15/96.

SWEEPSTAKES RULES

OFFICIAL RULES:

1. No purchase necessary.

2. To enter, complete this official entry form or hand print your name, address, and telephone number on a 3" x 5" card and mail to: Liftoff With the Trenchcoat Twins™, C/O Scholastic Trade Marketing Dept., P.O. Box 7500, Jefferson City, MO 65102-7500. Enter as often as you wish, but each entry must be mailed separately and received by October 15, 1996 for a late Fall 1996 visit to the U.S. Space Camp and Rocket Center. One entry per envelope. Partially completed entries or mechanically reproduced entries will not be accepted. Sponsors assume no responsibility for lost, misdirected, damaged, stolen, postage-due, illegible or late entries. All entries become the property of the sponsor and will not be returned. Odds of winning depend on number of eligible entries received.

3. Sweepstakes open to residents of the United States, children no older than 14 as of October 30, 1996, except employees of Dualstar Entertainment Group, Inc., WarnerVision Inc., Parachute Press, Inc., Scholastic Inc., U.S. Space and Rocket Center, their affiliates, subsidiaries, respective advertising, promotion, and fulfillment agencies, and the immediate families of each. Sweepstakes is void where prohibited by law.

4. Winners will be randomly drawn on or about October 30, 1996, by Scholastic Inc. whose decisions are final. Except where prohibited, by accepting prize, winner consents to the use of his/her name and photograph or likeness by sponsors for publicity purposes without further compensation. Winner will be notified by mail and will be required to sign and return an affidavit of eligibility and liability release within 14 days of notification attempt, or the prize will be forfeited and awarded to an alternate winner.

5. Grand Prize: A three (3) day, two (2) night trip for a parent and child (2) to a weekend session at the U.S. Space and Rocket Center (date of trip to be determined by sponsor by 10/30/96) to see a shuttle launch and meet the Olsen twins. Shuttle launch subject to availability. Not responsible for changes in NASA flight schedules, inclement weather or other delays/cancellations. Children must be between the ages of 7 and 14 to attend.If winner is unable to attend on specified date, winner can select an alternate date, without the Olsen twins' visit or the shuttle launch. Includes round-trip coach air transportation from airport nearest winner's home to the U.S. Space and Rocket Center, three (3) nights U.S. Space Camp lodging and meals. (Est. retail value $2,500). Grand prize winners must utilize prize within twelve (12) months subject to flight accommodations availability.

6. Prizes are non-transferable, not returnable, and cannot be sold or redeemed for cash. No substitutions allowed. Taxes on prizes are the responsibility of the winner. All federal, state, local laws apply. By accepting prizes, winners agree that Dualstar Entertainment Group, Inc., WarnerVision Inc., Parachute Press, Inc., Scholastic Inc., U.S. Space and Rocket Center, and their respective officers, directors, agents and employees will have no liability or responsibility for any injuries, losses or damages of any kind resulting from the acceptance, possession or use of any prize and they will be held harmless against any claims of liability arising directly or indirectly from the prizes awarded.

7. For a complete set of rules, or winners list, send a self-addressed stamped envelope by December 30, 1996 to: Liftoff With the Trenchcoat Twins™, C/O Scholastic Trade Marketing Dept., P.O. Box 7500, Jefferson City, MO 65102-7500.

© 1996 Dualstar Entertainment Group, Inc., Dualstar Video, The Adventures of Mary-Kate & Ashley, Mary-Kate + Ashley's Fun Club, Clue and all logos, characters, names and other distinctive likenesses thereof are the trademarks of Dualstar Entertainment Group, Inc., except U.S. Space Camp is registered and owned by the U.S. Space and Rocket Center. NASA name and logo used with permission of the National Aeronautics and Space Administration at George C. Marshall Space Flight Center. All rights reserved.